Clint Faraday
book 23
Dead Slow

Clint, Judi and Dave are going in from fishing near the Zapatillas. There is a group of tour boats ahead that are barely moving. A man calls that they have to proceed at dead slow.

A couple are in a boat ahead with the police surrounding them. Dead slow is as fast as they will ever go again – but *how* did they die? If they can discover that maybe they can find *why* they died. It was obviously not a natural death. Was it a paranormal killing – or a more direct form of murder?

Contents

About the author

CD Moulton has traveled extensively over much of the world both in the music business, where he was a rock guitarist, songwriter and arranger and in an import/export business. He has been everything from a bar owner to auto salvage (junkyard) manager, longshoreman to high steel worker, orchid grower to landscaper, tropical fish farmer to commercial fisherman. He started writing books in 1983 and has published more than 350 books as of January 1, 2023. His most popular books to date are about research with orchids, though much of his science fiction and fantasy work has proven popular. He wrote the CD Grimes, PI series, and the Det. Nick Storie series, Clint Faraday series, and many other works.

He now resides in Gualaca, Chiriqui, Panamá, where he writes books, plays music with friends, does research with orchids and medicinal plants. He has lately become involved in fighting for the rights of the indigenous people, who are among his closest friends, and in fighting the extreme corruption in the courts and police in Panamá.

He offers the free e-book, *Fading Paradise*, that explains what he has been through because of the corruption.

CD is the discoverer of the Chadam Protocol for curing cancer.

Facebook page Ambrosia peruviana for cancer.

Clint Faraday: Dead Slow

<u>*Heading Home*</u>

Clint Faraday called to Judi Lum, his attractive Oriental next door neighbor here in Bocas del Toro, Bocas Town, Panama, that there seemed to be a problem ahead. There were a gaggle of tour boats that seemed to not be moving.

Dave, their nutty botanist/musician friend, the third member of the fishing party in Clint's boat, said there were some police boats ahead of them.

They came closer, where Maxie, a tour guide with a party of snorkelers aboard, called that they had to proceed at dead slow. There was some kind of police problem ahead. Clint waved and set the motor back to idle speed, which is as fast as everyone was going. He got a melacatón from the cooler and sat back to chat with Judi and Dave about the run of tuna they hadn't managed to get into.

"The weather's not right for them to come in this close," Dave suggested. "It's too mixed. They bite when it's more steady. Low pressure isn't good for fishing.

"It was a nice day to be out here, though. No regrets!"

"It was nice," Judi agreed. "It's good to just go out and laze around, sometimes.

"I wonder why the police are out here. There's Sergio, so it's not a good sign."

Sergio Valdez was head of violent crimes in Bocas Town. Clint often worked with the police. As a retired detective from Florida, he had a lot of experience with the kinds of things that were just beginning to appear in Bocas.

They came abreast of the police boat and Clint went to talk with Sergio.

"It seems two people are dead. The boat was close against the mangroves there and people noticed it this morning when they went out for the tours. Guillermo called when he was coming in, and they were still there. They were down inside, and couldn't be seen. He thought maybe it was a stolen boat the thieves tied to the mangroves, after they took everything of value out. Esteban came out and called to say there were two bodies in the boat, on the floor.

"Clint, they might have died from some kind of poison or something. They weren't beaten or shot or stabbed or anything we can find. They aren't contorted, in any way. It's like they're asleep, more than dead. Very peaceful, in a way.

"I don't know if it's something for us or just for some other ... I'll have to wait until Doc tells me if it was a natural death.

"I would almost believe it was one of those suicide pact things, where they killed themselves because of cancer or something, but we have no note. They always leave that. It just seems so weird. I have a bad feeling about something this strange."

They talked a bit more, then went on to Bocas and to their houses. Judi was going to Panamá City in the morning, and Dave was going to Cusapín with his botanical research, so Ben and Earl, neighbors and friends, would take care of the plants they all had around.

Clint would wait until morning to check with Sergio and Doc to see if he would be needed.

Clint was up before dawn, as almost always. He fixed coffee and made a cheese omelet, then relaxed in his hammock on the deck for a few minutes, went for a swim, then went inside to put on some clothes. He never wore anything until he decided what he was going to do that day.

He checked his e-mail and erased the thirty one spam messages. He didn't need any enlarger or Cialis or lottery winnings or other silly scams. He wondered if they would ever stop those. He didn't think anyone was stupid enough to answer them anymore, but the number he received every day said different. Would people ever develop the intelligence to know their bank or the wife of the ex-president of Ghana or Yahoo! or anyone else who was giving away millions of dollars would never use the internet or your e-mail to tell you about it? In the spam section, no less? Were there people that stupid?

Stupid was asking such a ridiculous question. Anyone with the IQ of a rock would know better than to answer them, and they wouldn't be sitting there. They were there. Come to your own conclusions.

Judi called across the water from her deck to say she was on the way to the airport. She'd see him next week.

Ben and Earl came by to get her keys so they could take care of the plants. They came back, and Clint poured coffee for them. Earl was a Cordon Bleu chef. He invited Clint to a special dinner that night. There were going to be several people, including an attractive girl from Sweden Clint might find interesting.

Ben and Earl were gay, and considered themselves married. They knew Clint liked a certain kind of woman, so had invited her over.

"She's actually very intelligent, as well as very beautiful," Ben explained. "I know you don't like airheaded bimbos. Inga is here on a grant from the national university in Sweden, studying natural medicinal things. Dave will like her, but he's too involved with Selma right now, so doesn't fool around."

"Dave's going to Cusapín today, so won't be around, anyhow. Medicinal plants ... he knows a lot about that stuff from the Indigeno medicine people," Clint replied.

"Yeah! We told her you were our Ngobe friend, and that you'd be able to help her with the research," Earl said. "She's expecting to meet a Ngobe we told her was a real attraction to the women!"

"I *am* a Ngobe."

"Yes, but she's expecting one of those gods from the mountains or something, not a gringo," Ben pointed out. Clint gave him the finger. He had been declared a Ngobe by the councils, the second person to ever be so honored.

They chatted a bit, then Clint decided to go into town to see what was learned about the bodies in the boat. Maybe Doc had a cause of death for him, by now. He walked back toward town with Ben and Earl until they turned in at their house.

He stopped at the Golden Grill to chat with a few of the regulars there. Not too much was new, except that prices were beginning to get out of hand on the island. They went up about five percent recently on the mainland side, and the merchants used that as an excuse to raise their prices from thirty to sixty percent.

"Nobody will shop on the island anymore," Jim said. "We all get together to take one of our boats to Almirante once a week and buy everything there at half what we have to pay here. I don't see how they stay in business!"

"The tourists. They come from Europe and the states, where the prices seem to be the same. They used to say things were so cheap here, now they say the prices are about like at home," Harry said. "I'm in Dolega and David, most of the time, and they still can't believe how cheap everything is there. You meet them after they've been in Bocas and they shrug and say Bocas is a tourist trap. That's how they all are. It doesn't ever dawn on them that if people would refuse to pay those prices they would come down in a heartbeat. A tourist trap has to have one thing to stay in business."

"Yeah. Tourists," Travis said. "It looks like the more they have to pay here, the more they come here. They come and cry that everything was so expensive in Costa Rica that they left. At least it's still cheaper here than there."

In other words, same old same old, as to the

conversation.

Clint went to the police station and talked with Esteban and Emilio, then went in to Sergio's office.

"Damn it, Clint! Doc can't find any cause of death! There's nothing in the food or drinks still on the boat, and there isn't any physical reason they died that he can find. He's sending a lot of samples to Panamá City. They have much better equipment.

"I'm checking on them as much as I can. They came here from France, but they were born in England. Hartfordshire. They lived in Wisconsin, in the states, for nine years, then went back to England for one, then went to France for three years before coming here. They were planning to lease a place on the mainland, just out of Punta Robalo.

"I'll let you know what we find – if we find anything."

Doc came into the office. He'd come from the morgue where he hadn't gotten any answers. It seemed they went out there, tied to the mangroves and laid down to die. They were possibly alive when Guillermo went out, but were dead an hour or so later.

"I can't find any hint of normal deaths, but there's also no hint of an abnormal death. It's getting to me!"

"Well, I'm going to the Bahia. They were staying there, and the room was sealed when we found their bodies out there," Sergio said. "I haven't had time to go there yet, and didn't want to send the team without me along. Maybe Clint will want to come along. He's educated in CSI processes and techniques."

"Might as well. Can't dance," Clint replied.

Doc said he'd come along. Maybe there would be some clue in their room. They climbed into the police truck and headed for the hotel.

Voodoo?

Sergio got the room keys at the desk, then the trio headed up to the room. The team would be there in about ten minutes to do a more thorough investigation.

"Okay. Before we go in, let's be sure we know the things we've already learned about them," Doc suggested. "They were Elinor Diane Glesson-Partridge, thirty six years of age, five feet five inches and one nineteen pounds, and her husband, John Handly Partridge, thirty five years, six one and one eighty four. They were in France when they came here. They were planning to stay here for a period of no less than a year. That's the length of the lease they were trying to obtain.

"From what I've learned so far, they had met a number of people, both local and tourists, and were considered as good tourists, being likable people of more than average intelligence.

"She had worked in the past as a hotel manager in England, a hostess in a fancy restaurant in the states, and as a receptionist at a resort spa near Versailles, France. She hasn't worked for two years.

"He was a chemical engineer, working with plastics, acrylics, and agricultural chemicals. He was here to see if it would be practical to open a consulting agency that would practice in Central America and northern South America. He has made some discoveries, and held patents on two valuable processes with plastics.

"As I said, and this is with very limited input, to this point, they were both considered amiable and intelligent. They drank very moderately and watched their diets to maintain good health. I've seen a short transcript of their physical and medical history, and found they were naturally healthy people who were careful, though not to the extremes some reach, about diet and exercise, as well as exposure to too much sun and that kind of thing. The only drugs they ever used were marijuana, and that very seldom. A glass of red wine and a couple of tokes every four months for the benefit to the eyes. That was prescribed because she might be prone to retinal damage and glaucoma. Her mother was legally blind at forty five. Genetic uncertainty, and they were practical.

"There is nothing to suggest they were having problems, emotionally or financially.

"A solely personal feeling is that they were murdered. I have no evidence to back that up, except the circumstances surrounding their deaths.

"Anybody have anything to add?"

"That's a bit more complcte than what I have to the moment," Sergio replied. Clint shook his head.

"We don't have a starting point. We don't even have a point that points to a starting point," Doc said sourly. "If we can find how they were killed, we might be able to trace backward. I don't like that chemical engineer thing. We have to know who he knew or had trouble with or whatever in the chemical field, I fear. There's always a new way to kill people being developed, and some are damned near impossible to trace."

"Something occurs to me," Clint said. "I'll have to check on it, but it seems the main ones who develop new ways to kill off people are government programs."

"If it's that, they were working as undercover agents or something. We have to find which government and what they were working on," Sergio agreed sourly. "That would mean a very concentrated coverup."

"All we can do is investigate possibilities, for now," Clint said. "I'll have my sources check into them. There are always things that let you know if it's that crap. If it's that, I want to know what they were after."

"Definitely!" Sergio said. "Shall we go inside and try to learn something?"

"Yeah. That would be nice," Doc replied. They opened the door and went in.

The room was neat, but the maid had cleaned it since they left, before daylight. There weren't many possessions there, beyond the normal clothes and cosmetics and such people carried when they traveled. They hadn't left anything in the hotel safe. Clint noted their passports weren't in the room, and weren't in the safe, and weren't with them on the boat, though there was a copy of their passports in the room. That meant they had the passports in safe storage somewhere and, as suggested by the government, simply carried copies. Passport theft was, while not rampant, not a rare thing, either.

"They have things stored somewhere. They were looking to lease a place for a year," Sergio pointed out. "I'll get the input manifest from the aduana ... they came in through Frontera. Maybe we can trace where they stored the possessions. I will not be surprised either way if there is or isn't something there. I'll also trace back through the companies using his patents."

"I'll want to know what kinds of things he was working with," Clint said. "It'll be there. The reason ... we have to find who had a reason to kill them. Without motive, this kind of thing is next to impossible.

"What's this?" He picked up a little doll made out of straw. It had real hair.

"Let me see. I've seen this kind of thing before, but not here. It was with some people from the Dominican Republic. It's voodoo magic."

"I had a weird case where a witch woman was more or less pitted against the Indio medicine woman and some kind of real estate agent or something, over by Calderas (Book 8: *Omen*)," Clint said. "The CIA was involved – and I mean in both ends of that deal. You remember that, Sergio."

"Yes. Judi was kidnapped, the woman and her daughter were kidnapped, people got shot (Book 7: *Comedy of Terrors*). It was purely stupid. Panamanians don't put much stock in voodoo. Well, except the blacks originally from Jamaica and Haiti and those islands."

"No. The case where those people were running a scam on people about pirate treasure in the comarca. The witch woman in the kidnapping case was some voodoo queen or whatever they call them who wanted to take over the finances of the world, or something as silly."

"I've seen things that would curl your hair with that stuff, but most of it's psychological or poisons and drugs," Doc said. "There is a lot that can't be explained with what we know today, though. We must proceed with caution here!"

"You don't believe in that stuff, do you?" Sergio asked.

"No. I don't disbelieve it, either. Not all of it.

"What bothers me is their use of poisons and drugs. That's medical, and I damned well know how it works! You have to remember that some of those things will penetrate the skin very rapidly, and the least trace can be fatal. There are insecticides that will penetrate the skin and be absorbed."

"EDTA," Clint agreed. "It can carry even heavy metals through the skin."

"But I can find that quickly. It wasn't there. That's not to say another penetrant wasn't used. The plastics part makes it likely that they were in contact with things such as methyl-ethyl ketone peroxide, which can cause penetration and is poisonous, in itself. I can trace that, too. It's not here."

"Well, we know that something's involved, probably about plastics, probably some government, possibly voodoo, though that kind of doll is more the kind you stick pins in and so forth. It's probably just a tourist thing they bought somewhere," Clint mused. "I won't forget about it, but I won't concentrate on it, either."

Doc took a magnifying lens from his pocket to study the doll. He finally said, "I'd say that would be a terrible mistake. I have to check to be certain, but there are two types of hair on this thing. They would seem to be the hair of our victims. This is not anything they bought somewhere as a curiosity!"

"Then something special would have to be done to the doll," Sergio suggested. "Wouldn't that leave marks?"

"If it was stuck with pins or something such," Doc agreed. "If the doll is made ... I just don't have enough knowledge of this kind of thing to be able to say ... anything."

"I think I might know someone who can tell us!" Clint exclaimed. "I met her in two cases. She's out near the comarca past Chiriqui Grande."

"But will she?" Sergio asked.

"Yes. She's more like a medicine woman who knows something about voodoo because of the poisons and so forth they use."

"You check on that. I'll try to trace his business deals. Maybe it's a combination of things. Doc can try to trace what was used. It may be a thing Panamá needn't be bothered with, past keeping anyone who would use such methods out."

"I remember the time I would go after a killer merely on general principles and see that he was prosecuted. Now I'm forced to agree with a few of them," Clint said. "I've arranged for several to get out."

"It's not so rare a case here," Sergio agreed. "The motives are different than in the states. Too often, the motive is self-protection or protection of the family. Clint, you consider yourself a Ngobe. You protect them as your family. It's basic to their culture. You protect the Panamanian people almost as much. You arrange for those from other places to escape to where they can handle the source of the problem when we can't reach them. That's simple pragmatism. No one who actually did anything got away with it. When it's some government thing, I feel they're interfering with this country. I want that stopped! If it means turning their own creations against them, so be it!

"Are you going to Chiriqui Grande?"

"Yes. I'll ... not yet. Dave's in Cusapín, and knows the people. He can get the information for us. I'll concentrate on his plastics background. I want to know all about his patents."

Doc and Sergio both nodded. They discussed it a bit more, then Clint headed for his house. Dave would be on the computer soon after he arrived at

Cusapín. Maybe the voodoo woman there had a computer. He didn't believe this was a killing through voodoo. There was something solid and scientific behind it, both as to method and means.

"Olafia? That voodoo woman fifty feet outside of the comarca?" Dave asked. "You have two dead bodies who were probably killed with a voodoo doll?

"Gimme a break!"

They were using Skype. It was better than the cell phone here, because the signal was more steady.

"Dave, this is a weird one. We have the doll. It's made using their hair. We can't find what killed them. We can't find motive. It's a mess, and the only connection, no matter how vague, is that doll. To this point, that's our case!"

"You get some weird ones. I'll be able to get Silvio or Andres to run over there and ask her. I think she does have a comp that she uses to research natural medicinal plants. She's intelligent.

"Did you know that she gets along with the Indios, now that you showed she wasn't the one who was doing the nasty little things to them?"

"Yes. Basilio told me. There's just a natural suspicion between Indios and Blacks to overcome. She doesn't hold with a lot of the Black ideas, and Basilio doesn't hold to some of the Indio prejudices."

"The Indios aren't prejudiced. All they needed was to know it wasn't her, it was those others who were trying to make them believe it was her. I'll send Andres over. He's just coming in. Talk later!" He went off, so Clint went to the kitchen to prepare a ham and cheese sandwich. He would go back to the computer to try to trace the plastics connection as soon as he ate.

His comp dinged, about an hour later. He had an e-mail. From witchwomanolafiaone_ten.

Good afternoon Clint. I must know about the doll. It sounds as though it is one used more on the mainland. South Mexico to eastern coastal Nicaragua. Is the head hollow, and is there a grain of corn where the heart is? Is there a smell like rancid oil about it? Is there the spur of a rooster as a genital or a piece of iguana skin in the genital area? Is there a rice grain or small black pea behind where the eyes are, or used as eyes? This will tell me exactly where it came from. Perhaps that will answer your questions about who would use such a dangerous thing. The power of the doll can be turned back on the one who made or used it if the original motive was greed, making the user become consumed with greed even more. This is one of the three devices I fear. I cannot understand from whence the power emanates. It is nothing of science. It is the raw true voodoo from Africa. It necessitates a papaloi, not a witch. Take the greatest care! – Olafia

Clint read the message and printed it out, then headed as fast as he could for Sergio's office. He wanted to check that doll!

"It has both in the genital area," Doc reported. "It has one eye a black small pea and the other a grain of rice. The head is hollow. There are two small grains of corn for the heart. There is no smell of rancid oil. It's more like oregano. The hair is hers on the left and his on the right. The black pea is on the right eye. There is some kind of thread made from animal intestines woven into a pattern from the heart area to the top of the head, where there is a small crystal of some sort. It looks like a copper pyrite. There are small crystals – by small, I mean barely visible. I wouldn't have noticed if they weren't so carefully placed – on the big toes. There is a tiny needle made from a thorn of an acacia in each lung. If she needs anything more, tell me where to find it and an idea of what it is."

Clint sent that on. There was an answer five minutes later.

Good evening Clint. It is as I feared. This is a very powerful idol. The crystals tell me that they died from a combination of things, such as too much copper in the bloodstream. There will be concentrations of salts on the toes that you will consider incipient gout. The crystals are not uric acid. You will not be able to analyze them, because they will come apart very quickly and break down to other compounds. The dead people consumed something that had an extract from certain fishes and from certain other lifeforms from the sea. The death is timed very accurately from the ingestion of the poison to the time the crystals form. The needles in the lungs tell me the body was suddenly unable to absorb oxygen, much like cyanide works. The threads are from the intestines of a type of rock lizard. The poison works by suddenly depriving the body of oxygen and there is no discomfort. A person becomes very sleepy and may have a slight headache. The lungs are not distressed as with some such poisons. The person lays down and dies. The death stops certain hormone production and the compounds break down into water and natural organo-carbon compounds that occur naturally in the body. You would not be able to prove poison because there is nothing to detect after about two hours. The doll is somehow used

"Well, we have an area we can concentrate on, at least," Doc said. "I have to agree that we can never find anything to prove poison. I've used every test we have. It is true oxygen deprivation was a part of the death, and the copper content of the blood was somewhat excessive, but not directly fatal, but that is all.

"There is some kind of small dust that is very sharp on the doll, but it is part of the straw that makes up ... I think you can ask your witch woman if there must be a specific kind of straw that is produced through an exact program. We may be able to solve the delivery puzzle! I am very very damned glad we handle these things only with latex gloves! I have an idea we who handled that doll would become it's victims, had we not! I think the dust is much like the needles on fiberglass insulation. If you have any ex-perience, you will know that it penetrates any exposed skin and makes you itch like crazy for hours!"

"Sergio, who in Honduras or Nicaragua is in any way connected to them? We have to know. It'll answer our questions, if there's just one." Clint went to the computer to ask Olafia if there was such a process with the straw. The answer came back very shortly and positively.

Clint. The straw is from a kind of sawgrass that grows in swampy coastal areas. It is used in several kinds of dolls. I do not know how it is processed for use, but will know soon.

Clint sent back: *Olafia – the grass has a dust that Doc describes as being very sharp needles much like in fiberglass insulation. I believe we have the method of delivery of your poisons.*

He got a thanks, along with a promise that she would thoroughly investigate the method of producing the straw.

"Well, now we have to find out who might have connections among the indigenous people on a few small islands at the border of northern Honduras and Nicaragua," Sergio said. "Their passports weren't noted as being stamped from either place, I think."

"Then someone with a connection to them does have their passport stamped from those areas," Doc suggested. "I hope we can discover who, in our lifetimes. I think I will be able to find the straw fibers in their hands ... Clint! That doll was delivered at a specific time! It was delivered to the hotel, or was in their boat. The person who did this is here – or was yesterday! The rest of the things with the dolls is for distraction!"

Clint had to agree with that! "Well, I'll try to find who here had any contact with them, other than normal social interaction. If we can trace anyone to southern Honduras or extreme northern Nicaragua we'll have our first solid suspect!"

"I'll find them," Sergio promised. Doc said he was going to do the most thorough inspection and analysis on that particular straw that anything ever in history went through.

Clint headed for home. It was late enough that he would go to the places his killer might go to try to find a suspect. He wished Judi was there. She could get information in ten minutes it would take him hours to find.

They had a path to look ... no stupid cliches! He had a direction.

Doc called. The dust was cellulose fibers that were apparently produced on the straw, and was somehow processed to make it form into small hooked needles. The fiber needles were much harder than the other tissue of the straw, and were hollow. There was some kind of greyish gel in some of the needles. He didn't know how it was inserted.

"Doc, maybe it's because they contain the penetrant, and it inserts it automatically into capillary-sized tubes?"

There was a pause, then, "It would seem logical. Break the surface tension. Anionic detergent? There are a number of natural chemicals that can act that way. That would be found in the lizard intestine threads, and why there would be the odor of rancid oil. Possibly the acacia needle contains that. The oregano was added later, to confuse and cover the odor. We have discovered yet another way that voodoo and such things use to cause fear. It isn't magic or spirits, it's science."

"Well, as Dave always says, magic is simply science we don't understand – yet."

"Picture a fist with the middle finger extended. Later!"

Clint rang off and sat to think, then took a swim and SSS, dressed, and went to town. First, Gary's Mexican Restaurant, Gringos. He chatted with people, but learned nothing. He then went to Toro Loco, but there wasn't much going on. Natalie was still having all kinds of problems with the local legal system, but that wasn't the kind of thing he pretended to understand. Next was the Rip Tide. He was told that there was a man asking about him earlier, a sort of indistinct man who was average in an average sort of way. He was wearing a grey sports suit, which made him out of place, to a small extent. People, except lawyers, didn't wear suits here, to any extent.

Clint wondered. That said a lot more than most would hear. It smacked of CIA or such. They always *almost* blended, but almost always didn't quite make it. Maybe he was a lawyer where he came from, and the lawyer thing would fit, but why would a lawyer from someplace else want to meet him?

He left and went to El Ultimo Refugio for a beer and to chat with people. The described man was there, and came directly to him to ask if he could have a word. Clint shrugged, and they went out front.

"I'm Gerald Winston. I'm with the CIA, in a way, but am also into other things.

"What I want to know is what's going on in the Partridge case?

"I don't want anyone to know I have a special interest in it. There may be nothing there for me. We've watched him for awhile, because of the plastics patents he held. They weren't anything that would hold our interest. They were more things like a plastic for automobile dashboards and such that wouldn't come apart in a few years from sunlight and a material a lot like PVC that wouldn't deteriorate from light exposure. They were very profitable breakthroughs, to an extent, but of little use in military matters. That's the thrust of my connection with the CIA. That, and drugs coming in through here and Honduras.

"You see the problem. Why were he and his wife killed? There has to be something, and it could be because he's developed something with military application."

"We haven't found a clue as to what it was about. We did find the method, but not the motive."

"You found the method? Other than voodoo?"

"It was voodoo, but now we've explained it scientifically. To these people, it's voodoo. To us, it was poison with a very clever delivery system. It was a chemical that caused sudden oxygen deprivation. It was delivered by a voodoo doll."

"I suppose your medical examiner can explain it to our people. I don't have a clue as to what you mean.

"Mr. Faraday, I'll greatly appreciate it if you will keep me informed if there is *anything* about this that comes under our interests."

"I'll promise to tell you anything I learn that's in the area of your business. I won't tell you anything that I don't consider the business of government intrusion into people's lives for the sole sake of intruding into people's lives. Fair enough?"

"I think I like you, Clint Faraday! I'll break the rules, in that I'll tell you anything I learn that could help your case. I know from experience what kinds of excesses the US government goes to to monitor its citizens."

"I wouldn't give a shit how much they intrude themselves into their own people's affairs, if the people will put up with the crap. I do care about them intruding outside of their borders in the ways they do."

"We agree in that. I thought this would be an exciting job, where I would be protecting the country and people, not a bunch of bankers."

"And power crazy politicians." They shook hands, and Winston bought Clint a beer. This was the third CIA agent he'd met here who thought the intrusion of government into people's lives had gone much too far.

Of course, he also knew not to trust what they projected, to any extent. He wasn't *that* naive.

Clint went for his morning swim and climbed out onto his deck to rinse in the shower there, then went inside to shave and clean up, then put on the day's uniform, shorts and a tee shirt and chankletas.

First item on the agenda was to find someone he could connect with the Partridges in more than a vague peripheral way. Maybe someone who had been in Honduras or Nicaragua.

He thought about it, then called Sergio: "Sergio, find out about that boat. I have a few questions that could be answered by where that boat's been."

"Yes. Like the Caribbean islands north of here. It wasn't the type of boat usually used for those distances, but it's not a difficult trip, only a bit uncomfortable. The boat is designed for day, and maybe one night, use."

"My idea is something along a different line. Maybe we should be looking for someone who came on a boat."

"I see. A boat that could well have moved among certain of the Caribbean islands without drawing attention and without getting a passport stamped, perhaps?"

"Just get a list of the possibilities. I'll try to get enough information to tie someone into this."

"Will do!"

He called Judi and asked that she come back to Bocas. He would make it up to her. He explained what he needed. There was no one in the world who could get critical information faster and more complete than Judi Lum.

He spent the rest of the day learning a little more about the voodoo end and looking into what he could find about Partridge and plastic patents.

The patents were for things like Winston had suggested. The main thrust was toward producing a fairly cheap and usable plastic that wouldn't deteriorate in sunlight, that was easy to clean, that wasn't affected by water or solvents, and was easy to mold in ways that would retain their size and form for long periods. The uses were mostly for, as suggested, automobile interiors and water/liquid delivery tubes and tanks. It seemed there was no big secret about anything he was doing. He had the patents, and was making a moderately good living on the royalties. The processes didn't require much retooling, and use was growing.

That seemed usual and along the general lines

of commercial processes. It wouldn't have any particular advantage to military items. Had he found a CIA agent who actually was honest with him?

He remembered that Sergio had suggested that a government operation would have very good and very solid coverup in place. It was just that nothing here seemed to apply to that end of the way of the world.

Judi came in on the four thirty flight and he went into an intense explanation of what he needed, which was mostly who had been to those specific Caribbean islands. He could probably find out by his methods, but that would alert the subjects about what he was after. Judi could get the information faster and more accurately by avoiding the subject. She had tried to teach Clint how to do it. He had been able to get part of it right, but he needed all of this right.

It wasn't so much that he wanted to solve the case. He always wanted that. He wanted to know why, and that there wouldn't be others drawn into something nasty through no fault of their own.

Doc called just at dinnertime to say Olafia had sent him the process for making the straw figures. It was successful because the straw produced almost a scaling eddect of cellulose scales. The process removed the softer tissue and caused the scale to form a tube as it dried, by drying one side faster than the other, a process that fascinated him. He said it had some very important methods included that could make someone millions if they could adapt it to commercial use. The poison was inserted by dissolving it in an aloe vera based liquid that would act as a surface tension reducer and dry into a gel that didn't affect the poison, itself. It actually preserved it, and formed the penetrant when the body liquids were absorbed by the gel. The straw was only found among those islands, some small islands off Australia, and some bay islands along the Atlantic coast of mid-Africa..

They had everything but why and who.

Sergio called to say that the personal property of the Partridges was in a commercial storage facility in Changuinola. He had made arrangements for Clint and he to go there the next morning to open it. Maybe they could get some answers there.

Clint met a pretty girl from Hawaii and spent the whole evening with her. Judi called just after midnight and said she might have found who he was after. She would stop at his place on her way home. Ten minutes.

Maybe this would come together.

Judi came in to say she had talked with almost

all the people he had listed as coming in boats. Most of them were drinking at the old marina bar and restaurant. She had Quint, an Indio friend who kept a boat there, take her to dinner so she could show him off. He was very handsome and the type of person people automatically liked. The women, particularly gringas, were very much attracted to him.

Harry Morisson had come down the Pacific coast and through the canal. He was on the way to Rhode Island in about a month. Glenna and Bob Finders had come along the coast from Texas, and had stopped at Rotan. in Honduras. It was too touristy for them, something that was true about Bocas Town. They hadn't been to any of the other islands, which was probably a big mistake. Maybe if they went to the unknown ones they would find something they could relate to.

That could be a coverup. There was no way they could be checked easily. Check them out.

Larry Goodman had stopped at Rotan, but didn't know about the other islands. He had let it slip later that he sort of liked Utila, so he had moved among the lesser islands. He had later let it slip that he went to La Ceiba to shop before coming on where he met some narcos from the states. He was the top suspect now!

Norman and Winifred Parks hadn't made many

stops. Only for fuel and some food supplies. They were only on the big islands farther north and south. Winifred had said something about the lobster being fished out of the inner waters along the Mosquito Coast, which meant they were definitely among the smaller islands in question. Suspect(s) two.

George and Elaine Waters hadn't come to that area. They came around west of Cuba and down among the islands and in at the canal. They had a big catamaran. They used the sails, mostly. It wasn't an easy craft to maneuver among those closer islands.

No one else there.

Quint took her to Carenero, where she met one other. Knowles was the only name he had used. He had come along the coast from Louisiana and had spent a lot of his time among all the coastal islands.

That narrowed the field! Knowles, the Parks, and Goodman were the top, with the Finders second best bet. Now if they could find any one of those names in that storage unit they could close in fast.

In the morning Sergio called to say someone had tried to get access to the storage bin around midnight last night. The guard saw him, a single man, and ran him off.

Damn! All the suspects were close to Judi around midnight and not long before. It was getting muddier again.

Was there time for someone to go from the Bocas marina to Changuinola before midnight?

He called Judi. Goodman and the Parks might have, if they had a car in Almirante and a fast boat. She had talked with them earliest. Knowles was out.

Wasn't he? "Judi, was Knowles traveling alone, or with someone?"

"I don't know. That's a possibility, isn't it?"

He called Sergio to ask if Knowles came alone.

"Knowles?"

"Carenero. Has a boat."

"Just a minute." There was a pause, then, "No. He's traveling with Edgar Levanthal."

Suspect number one! "Thanks, Sergio. I think we might be able to concentrate on Knowles and Levanthal."

"It was Levanthal at the storage unit?"

"It's possible to the point of probable that he was the one. We'll have to investigate those two.

"I'll be around in my boat in a few minutes and we can see if we can find what they want in that storage unit."

He finished what he was doing, took Judi to the airport to catch her flight back to her visit, then took his boat around to the police dock to board Sergio and Emilio. They were in Almirante three quarters of an hour later. Sergio checked the records at the bus terminal. Levanthal hadn't produced ID there for anywhere – which meant nothing. ID's were checked only when they booked a ride in advance.

If he took a water taxi, they had the ID listed. He went with Sergio and found Levanthal had come to Almirante yesterday about three o'clock. He hadn't gone back to Bocas Town on a water taxi.

They drove to Changuinola in Clint's car. He asked that Emilio check at the airport to see if Levanthal went anywhere else. He had gone to Las Tablas an hour ago.

"He was here at midnight."

"He put on his flight reservation that he was staying at the Gran Central," Emilio suggested. They went there. Levanthal was in his room from ten fifteen until five this morning.

"Shit!" Clint cried. "There goes suspect number one!"

"No. He went to his room at ten and checked out at five. Where he was in between is not established. All he had to do was take his key with him and no one who didn't see him would know if he was there or not. It is perhaps less likely that he is our prime suspect, but it doesn't change the equation much."

Clint had to agree with that. It made the case a bit deeper. It was already muddy. Maybe that storage unit would give them an answer or two. He could hope!

They went to the storage unit and used the keys from the hotel to remove the padlock. The second padlock had already been cut. They took pictures and printed the door and both padlocks, but didn't entertain any idea that would tell them anything. No one was stupid enough to not wear gloves for that sort of thing.

There was some furniture in the unit, and some clothing. There were several steel filing cabinets with both key and combination locks. They had the keys, but needed the combinations. Sergio smirked and took the little address book from his pocket.

"This was taught to me by a gringo detective who works with the police at times in Bocas. The combinations are four numbers. These addresses are not what we want, I would tend to think. The telephone numbers are.

"You will note that there are four filing cabinets along with four numbers with a fax code. The fax codes do not match with the telephone numbers."

"So we have to determine which code goes with

which cabinet," Emilio suggested. "The keys have a number scratched into each, one through four. I would say the number one key is to the first fax code."

Sergio tried all the keys on the first cabinet. It was number three. He used the number three combination, and it opened.

"Elementary, my dear Clinton," Sergio said, getting the finger.

The file was mostly research papers for the processes patented. There wasn't much else there.

The second was number one. It was receipts and records of costs in researching the patents and developing the process.

Number three was the patent records, themselves, and the ones who were paying royalties.

Number four was general office records.

"It's boredom time," Sergio announced. "We can each take a file and look for ... what, besides the names, Clint?"

"The names are most important. Dates attached to the names are next. What the receipt or whatever is about is third. We'll have to make a code for that process. Maybe 'A' for research, 'B' for royalties ... that will get too complicated. First, names and dates. This file will probably give more than a hundred dates for twenty names or something. If you come across ... I'll be damned! He has that listed in a folder, the first one. All I have to do is look for a name we've come across here! We can try to match to any names here in the past four days!"

"Most of these are company names. The list is here. There's also a list of who represents each company," Emilio said. "This guy makes things a lot easier than I would have thought!"

They went through the lists, but didn't find any matches with their major suspects.

"The office records won't be listed so well," Clint complained. "We'll have to read the top or signature or something on all of this."

They spent almost an hour cross-checking the correspondence. Suddenly, Emilio cried, "Here it is! You'll never guess who!"

"Leventhal or Knowles?" Sergio asked.

"The Parks would be the least suspected of our little group, so them," Clint said.

"No! Goodman! He was asking about outright purchase of one of the patents. He later was seeking a partnership that Partridge refused."

"It still doesn't make sense for him to kill them!" Sergio cried.

"We have to find the reason. It just gets deeper and muddier everywhere we go. We have the murders, the connection, the opportunity, the method. We don't have a hint of motive with this, unless a partnership was actually formed," Clint explained. "We know who did it, how he did it, when he did it. We just don't have *why* he did it, and we can't get a conviction on this kind of thing without that. It might be hard *with* that!"

"Then we'll have to learn why," Sergio said. "Let's go through this one more time to be sure there isn't something that would give Goodman or anyone else a profit if they killed him. I can well do without more complications. I don't want to write this one off. It's a matter of the killer thinking he's smarter than are we. He's smirking at us. We'll have to wipe the smirk off of his face."

"We have another problem," Clint warned. "*Who* was trying to get into here at midnight? With this, it *wasn't* Levanthal!"

Sergio and Emilio looked at one another and shrugged. "Talk about deeper and muddier!" he complained. "Now we have to find a connection with Goodman and someone else here. Fuck!"

"I might have a suspicion and a suspect," Clint said slowly. "I just might!

"Let's get what we need here and go back to Bocas."

Clint finished his statement for the police and went home to clean up. He was going to see if someone would sniff around the bait he was going to leave there. Something had occurred to him. Something someone said and something Judi reported. It might connect two people through a thing that wouldn't seem to have any connection. It still remained to determine why the murder had taken place. It simply didn't seem to make sense. There seemed no logical way anyone could profit from Partridge's death.

That simply meant there was something they didn't know. Yet. It had to be connected with those plastics, but a new one he hadn't patented or an older one?

He saw Ben and Earl starting out, and walked along with them toward town. They were always around the tourists, and were popular. They might just be the ones to get the message he wanted around. He explained what he wanted.

"You see, if someone reacts to that, they'll give themselves away in ways they don't guess. Two can play that game. I don't think I could find a connection any other way."

"So. We say that there's some kind of drug connection they knew about, or something we don't understand. Drugs or a drug dealer or a narc. You seem to be going in ten directions at once. You found some strange things that need explaining in some hidden files somewhere. Maybe some kind of process to make drugs or something else vague. All this around the boat crowd," Ben said. "This is another one of your little subterfuges, isn't it?"

"Yes and no. It's partly true. I have to see how several people react. That'll tell me where the trouble came from. Maybe. I may be pissing up a rope, but it's all I've got."

"No problem. Anywhere else to spread the tale?" Earl asked.

"Anywhere anyone asks you anything about it. You can sort of let out that I seemed stoned or something on the way into town tonight, and kept babbling about the case. See who asks what."

"Particularly around the boat crowd," Ben said.

"Particularly," Clint agreed. "But *not* exclusively. I could be watching the wrong ones."

They parted just in town. Clint went to the Lemon Grass for Thai food, Ben and Earl went to The Pirate. After the delicious meal, Clint went to The Reef when he saw Goodman go in with a local (ahem) "lady." He sat at the bar on the end, close to where Goodman was seated, and had a beer, chatted with a couple of people about fishing and so forth, got some things said that Goodman would overhear, if not clearly, and went on to Refugio, then across to the Rip Tide, then to Toro Loco. He mentioned things at all the places. Ben and Earl had gone to the Barco Hundido, then across to Carenero.

About midnight Winston came in and waved carelessly. He soon gravitated to Clint and asked how the case was going. Clint said it was going dead slow, at the moment, but there may be a way to kick-start it. He had some information requests out.

"Well, it might be one of those things you can't figure. I know I can't, what with voodoo and all that stuff.

"Have you considered a drug connection? Everything here ends up there, anyhow."

"There's a connection, but it takes peripheral to the limit. Not serious, in itself, but for where it leads and who it leads to."

"Got a hint?"

"Oh, yeah! A couple of things."

Winston looked slightly confused, then hid it. "I wouldn't think there was any connection with them. From what we'd learned they wouldn't be stupid enough to get tied up with that crowd."

"It's not them. It's various others. Drugs are coincidental, at most. It's those drug dealers and investigations that put people in certain places at certain times."

"You lost me there."

"There are a lot of coincidental connections. More than one, and I'm suspicious. More than three, and I know it's bullshit.

"Oh, there's Nan! Have a good night!" He walked away to greet Nancy Foreman, a woman who lived out his way. He greeted her, and they went to the bar for a drink. Clint ordered a margarita for her, knowing that was her drink. They chatted awhile. Winston hung around about a half hour, then left. Clint smirked at his back. Nan asked why.

"He's CIA investigating something that's none of his business."

Nan was married to a CIA agent until he was killed, two years ago.

"He's not CIA. There's something he would have done if he was."

"I know that. I just wonder what he's up to. And why."

They chatted awhile, until George Vernon came in. Clint knew they were going together, and that he would come in, so said he was on his way, and left. He went to the Rip Tide, because it was on the way home. Winston was there, and tried to pump him to find what he was investigating. He said that, at the moment, he wanted to know where some boat people were at certain times.

"Boat people? Certain times? What will that tell you?"

"Nothing. Unless someone else was there at the same time."

That confused him even more.

Clint waited for one more beer to see if Winston had fallen for the trap.

"Uh, you were going to Changuinola. Find anything there?" Winston finally asked.

"Oh, furniture, clothes, files. Not a lot. Normal things."

"Files?"

"You know. The standard business records, research records, royalty contracts. That kind of thing."

"I guess the police can get an order and cut the locks to get in. They do have that advantage. It's too bad it didn't lead anywhere special."

"Cut the locks? Why?"

"Er, those units are double locked. We, er, knew about that from when we were investigating the military angle."

"We had the keys from the ring in the boat's

ignition. Why would we cut the locks? Someone else cut one of them, but that happens all the time here. The guard comes by often enough that it's damned rare for anyone to get in."

"Uh, I guess. The files had keys, too. That would be logical."

"Those were in his stuff at the hotel. He had the combinations listed in his address book."

"Have you discovered what it's about? Why they were killed?"

"I'll know that when I get some answers from the states. We have a number of requests out for information in several places." He remembered something from the expenses lists. "It'll be someone who worked with him, or was employed by him. He did use some people in the research end to do the gofer bit."

Bingo! Winston looked physically sick. Their quarry and the reason were concerned with someone who had worked for or with Partridge. That meant it was probably a new process that wasn't patented yet, but that would make a huge profit. The person who worked with him knew the process, and would file a patent on his own.

"Er, do you suppose someone knows about, I don't know, a new process or something, and wants to get it?"

"That would really be an exercise in futility! He

has exact and very detailed records of everything. If the patent hasn't already been applied for, it would give the killer away in a heartbeat!"

Now Winston looked more smug again. "I guess that would be too true. If he's killed, and suddenly someone wants a patent on his work, it would be as good as an admittance."

"Yes. Bye bye alibi! Well, got to run! See you!" Clint headed for home. He had it now, but would have to do some digging. It might be hard to prove, but this one wasn't going to get away Scot free. Someone had already applied for a patent. Partridge was killed because he could prove it was his process. It really was in those records!

Who had worked for him was also in those records. It wasn't Winston. Not under his real name.

Sergio had the files at the station. He would be there first thing in the morning. Maybe they could clear this mess up fairly fast. Winston was right about it being as much as admission of guilt if that process was patent pending already.

Clint called Sergio as soon as he was ready to go into town, which was before the station opened. Sergio would be there at seven thirty, when they would try to find the process. It would be the latest he was working on, or the one before. They would have to learn how to find what patents were pending in the field. Clint didn't doubt there were thousands. Maybe there was a good way to determine which one was their target quickly.

Sergio went to the computer and got the records from the patent office. He would use the (huge) list when they knew what they were looking for.

Clint got the records from the files, and found that a flexible plastic compound and process was discovered that would be very good for making plastic covers for driver's licenses and ID cards and so forth. It was clear, and shouldn't discolor from age or light exposure, and was hard enough that the things that generally scratched such things wouldn't scratch it. It was almost an acrylic, but remained flexible without interior distortion. It could be folded any number of times without tearing along the crease.

"This doesn't seem to be anything that anyone would kill over," Sergio said. "It will be useful, though. We could use it with the cedulas and carnets, and there wouldn't be the need to replace them every couple of years. The patent includes the machine that seals it. It uses heat and a type of solvent that actually makes the cover one piece.

"I don't think this is it. It will be a good idea, and will be used, but we're talking about a profit of ten cents per seal."

"A paper clip gives a profit of a fiftieth of a cent per. The originator is a multimillionaire," Clint pointed out. "How many cedulas would you use it on in a year, in this country, alone? How many countries? How many driver's licenses and social security cards and so forth? We're talking about something that, if the exclusive patent is given, will make a hundred million per year, after it's established, then the patent can be renewed or released to public use. I'd say the patent holder would make a billion dollars in the seven years of the original patent."

"Cripes!"

"How many new uses would come up? How many more billions would it make?

"It's the ignored little ten cent item that makes

the billionaires faster and more certainly than big multi-million dollar deals."

"Well, will it be Goodman or Winston or someone else?"

"That's the billion dollar question. We have to dig it out of these files, or get someone to lead us to him."

Clint took one folder and sat to study it. Sergio took another. They were looking for the name of anyone who worked for or with Partridge.

Sergio dropped the folder he was working with on the desk and took the computer to find who had applied for a patent of the process. He soon narrowed the net search to films, sheets, and coverings, plastic. There were seventy four, so he brought up the descriptions of the product, without trying to get the process itself. That wouldn't be given. He finally had it down to four that would fit, and had Clint see what he could find.

"This one is self-sealing with heat. It'll be like what's in use now. It's only advantage seems to be that it doesn't discolor as quickly. This one is for use in very cold climates, and seems a waste of money, to me, but what do I know. This one uses a retreatment every four years at virtually no cost to get the results of this one, which has to be it.

"The patent pending form has been applied for in the name of SuperbSealersInternational, S.A. We have to trace that one."

"It's an S.A. registered in Mexico. It'll be a rough deal to learn anything about it," Sergio replied. "I can give it a go!"

He sat at the computer and traced as far as he could on the net, SSISA was owned by DevDrim Something or Other which was owned by GoodKnightFabrics which was a corporation owned 90% + by Lawrence Oliver Goodman. Gerald Francis Winston was listed as 5% first vice president.

"Okay. I'm going to send the information on Partridge's process to the patent office. I'll explain that I believe it was stolen research where the man who developed the process has been murdered. I think that, just perhaps, your patent office will cooperate in helping us catch a murderer.

"That will leave us with the huge problem of determining which of them killed the Partridges."

"Either it was Goodman alone, for that part, or both of them," Clint replied. "Goodman is the one who took a boat to that island to get the poison. He's guilty, alone or equally with Winston, if Winston delivered the doll. Either way he's legally guilty of murder one. He can't bribe anyone here if he doesn't have that process. He doesn't have nearly the funds he would need."

"I think maybe we can see to it. This time, do not have him sent away to face justice elsewhere. This one is ours. He killed here."

"Agreed. Let's document all of this we can and get the show on the road!"

They spent more than three hours writing up and putting the evidence in chronological order. Finally they sat back. Sergio said, "Our one main problem will be proving that poison was used. There is no logical way it wasn't, but it leaves no trace."

"I think Doc can determine that. All he has to do is find those scales from the sawgrass in their skin."

"We can hope. Our courts are overly-endowed with corrupt and very clever lawyers. It is a lot like those more dramatic things from the states, where some trickery misdirects a judge or jury. If we can predetermine the trick, we can counter it."

"I know what would be tried in the states. I can counter it, because of another difference in such things here. A lawyer has to be very careful when he tries certain tricks. They can turn on him in a flash!

"We've spent enough time on this that it's as much as done. All I'm going to do is try to find how deep Winston is buried in the thing. If he delivered that voodoo doll, I want him to face the consequences. If not ... he's still accessory to the point he won't get away with anything.

"Have you found any heirs for that patent and his other things?"

"Yes. He has an older sister in England. He has houses in France and Wisconsin, and a condo in Miami. He also has a bank account of several millions of dollars. His sister raised a son he had with a previous wife who left him through a bitter divorce where she made a lot of extreme claims that he didn't bother to deny. He produced four men in the neighborhood who she was sleeping with and who said the things she claimed were false. He had DNA tests on the child, though he would have cared for him, regardless. It's his son. He's now sixteen years of age, and has his father's intelligence. He lived with them when they were in a place for any time. He is now with the sister, because of school. Had they found property here, he would have come. Partridge felt diversified schooling was to the child's benefit. He already speaks several languages fluently.

"Their wills left everything to the sister and son, except for ten thousand pounds to her first cousin in England, who is her only surviving relative she knows of. She was orphaned when she was nine years of age. She was raised from that time by the cousin, who is eleven years older, and whose mother was killed in the same traffic accident that killed Elinor's parents. Her father was deceased three years before then.

"They have all been notified. The sister has faxed the international crematory certificates to Doc. He is to have the process completed and will send the ashes to her. The ashes are to be spread in the sea. They always loved the water and boating.

"I think I'll want to know more about Winston before we arrest them. We will have to inform them that they cannot leave. That might make it necessary to arrest them too soon, but it is what we must do."

"I'll tell them they can't leave, and drop a few bombs on them," Clint replied. "Maybe we can get something from their reactions."

"Reactions to what?"

"Why, to the proven fact that they have to stay because they were involved in filing for a patent on one of his discoveries."

"That will tell them we know they're guilty. They'll try to run."

"Which will be proof enough for your courts here that they are guilty, and know they can't fight the conviction – which will result in their fast conviction."

"You always were sneaky. Let's see what we can dig up about Winston before we have to do that."

Sergio got the passport information from immigration, and they studied it carefully. He had traveled rather extensively for some suspicious companies.

"You know something? I think he might have actually been with your CIA!" Sergio suggested. "This kind of travel to these places hardly makes sense, otherwise."

"It's not my CIA. He's just not that professional about it. Nancy saw right away that he wasn't CIA. They have an identification code of some sort."

"He might be with some other agency."

"Or have been. One that operates inside the US. That would fit.

"You know something? I'll bet it's treasury! IRS! He looks for tax sources outside, among the ex-pats."

"That would lead to Partridge because? They were Brits."

"Who lived in Wisconsin, and who developed a process that was patented from the US. I think I want to know a lot more about friend Winston! I think ... I'll find that out fast!"

He called his ex-mob chief who was now living on Isla San Cristóbal. Clint had set it up to where he could escape the sad mobster lifestyle and raise a family who wouldn't be ashamed of what pop made his doing.

"Manny? I have to know a few things about a man named Winston who's involved in the Partridge murders. I think he was once an IRS agent who found ex-pats in other countries."

"Like they're doing here. I was warned about that, but they can't trace me. I don't get anything from the US anymore. It all stays there. Give me the name and something or other."

Clint passed the phone to Sergio, who gave all the information from the passport. Manny would call back in less than an hour. Sergio and Clint went to Subways to get a sandwich and coffee. Manny called back before they were through and reported that Winston was an ex-IRS agent who suddenly quit, three years ago. He was a typical agent, and there was very little suspicion of him, though Manny's sources reported that a person could arrange not to be found, for a fee. He may be using that story to find people who will believe he's out of it, or he may have found a source of income large enough that he didn't need the job.

"The latter," Clint said. "Thanks, Manny.

How're the wife and brat?"

"Fine! Driving me crazy, but that's a short trip!"

They chatted for a minutc, then Clint said he was about ready to inform friends Goodman and Winston they couldn't leave the island for the nonce.

Clint went home, cleaned up, dressed, and went back to town. He learned that Winston had gone to the Pickled Parrot on Carenero, so got his boat and went over. The chitras (sand flies) were bad, so he rubbed on some of the leaves from a plant the Indios gave him. It was a better repellant than the commercial things.

Winston was at the bar, talking with a local girl. Clint waved and grinned at him.

Goodman was at a table on the deck. He was also talking with a local girl.

There weren't many in the place. Clint went to the end of the bar and ordered a Balboa. He could see Goodman in the mirror. Goodman pointed to Clint and shrugged. Clint had excellent peripheral vision, and saw Winston shrug in answer.

What the hell! Clint walked over to Goodman and said, "Good evening, Mr. Goodman. I'm Clint Faraday. I'm involved in the investigation of the murder of the Partridges.

"It's a really nice evening. It's too bad the chitras are so active here, but the breeze will come up in a few minutes, and they won't be bad out here on the deck."

"Partridge? Those people found in the boat, killed by a voodoo curse or something?"

"Yes. The person whose big discovery you're attempting to patent."

He dropped his drink. Riata stared at him. She spoke very good English. He turned to look at Winston.

"Why not invite your vice president to join us? It's too nice a night to play stupid games that are already over."

"What the hell?!" he exclaimed. Clint waved to Winston, who set his face in a grim mold and came over to ask what was going on. Clint said the game had been fun, in a way, but it wasn't needed anymore.

"Okay. How did you find out? It's nearly impossible to trace those S.A.'s!"

"You aren't the only one who knows how to use the old voodoo techniques. I know a woman called Olafia who can find anything about anyone, anywhere, at any time. She combines voodoo and computers, believe it or not.

"Producing that doll involves a process that would be better than Partridge's, so far as making money goes."

"Really? Some voodoo woman claims that I'm involved in something, and the police act on it?

How interesting! Don't you think my profession would make me know the laws here?"

"An IRS agent? You would know the financial dodges, I suppose. You should concentrate on the computer angle more. Everything is somewhere on the net. It's a matter of knowing how to find it."

"IRS? I'm with – or was – CIA."

"Nancy's husband was CIA. You don't know any of the recognition sequence they use. You're not CIA. I don't need voodoo magic to discover the obvious. It took me two minutes to learn you were with IRS and suddenly quit about.... Wow! Just when Goodman applied for the patent! Talk about a coincidence!"

He and Goodman looked very uncertain.

"I just wanted to tell you you can't leave here for the time being. If you try, you'll be arrested, and have to sit in a cell. It's too nice a spell of weather to have to do that."

They didn't say anything. They exchanged a lot of uncomfortable looks. Clint said to have a pleasant evening, and went back to the bar, then got in his boat and headed back across the calm channel to the police dock. Sergio grinned, and said he saw the whole thing through his night vision binoculars.

"They'll try to run, you know," he warned.

"Let's see if they have the intelligence to not try it. I think they'll probably fall back to plan two or something."

"What do you think they'll do?"

"Winston has court experience in several countries, but it's not the kind of thing that will help them here. He only thinks it will. I think I know what they'll do. I planted the idea. Court could be a lot of fun, if they do."

"What do you mean?"

"Their lawyer will try for reasonable doubt. What he'll do will mean that they get a certain conviction if he does it, or as sure a conviction if he doesn't. Your lawyer can be your absolute worst opponent, here. Particularly if you haven't been truthful with him."

"The lawyer will try to appear an opponent?"

"No. It will turn one eighty on him when he tries his little trick. He wouldn't do it without their insistence

"You see, in the states, they would be honest enough with their lawyer that he would know better. Here? They have to lie a little, then have to admit the lie right there in court, or have some serious charges added. When this happens, they'll know they've left themselves with no hope and no way out – except maybe to turn on each other."

Sergio shook his head. "Maybe. They're getting the taxi. Their girlfriends seem to have deserted them – and it was going to be such a good night!"

"Well, it'll be an unique one, at least."

Goodman and Winston went to the water taxi station and walked toward the parque, followed at a distance by Sergio and Clint. They were in what was called a "very intense" conversation that involved arm waving and pointing. Winton went to the Tropical Suites, and Goodman went on into the parque and the public phones there. He called a number, then another. The second answered, and he said something and hung up, then went to sit on a park bench by the sidewalk. Sergio told Esteban to watch for Winston to run.

After about twenty minutes, Carlos Santeriana, a local lawyer, came to sit talking with Goodman. Clint worried that he might have miscalculated. Santeriana was pretty sharp.

Goodman went to the dock and took his dinghy back to his boat at the marina. Sergio had a man watching. If he tried to leave, he was going to get a hell of a surprise.

Clint said he was going home to sack out. They could arrest the two in the morning. He stopped at the Rip Tide for a beer, then went on home.

In the morning Sergio went with him and Emilio to arrest Winston for murder one. Esteban went with another officer to Goodman's boat to arrest him as being co-defendant. Sergio had the arraignment set and done in a few minutes, then he, Clint, Emilio and Esteban got together to put their case together. Clint didn't tell them what he thought might happen. He wasn't so sure, with Santeriana handling the case. They would have to wait. They probably had more than enough, already, but he hoped the trick would work to make it a very short case.

Santeriana came to say they wanted a speedy trial in front of a judge, and would waive a jury, who would very probably convict them simply because they were gringos. He smirked at Clint. Sergio said right now would suit him, if the judge was available, which shook the lawyer a bit. He asked if he could read over the case before court to see that there weren't any easily shown false-hoods or exaggerations. Clint had his copy, and handed it to him. He sat at a table while the rest of them chatted about fishing and the ongoing trouble with the government trying to take the Indio land. Clint used his peripheral vision to note when Santeriana read page two. There was a little mark by an item that looked like a question mark had been erased. He finished the page, and sat back. He said it seemed a very strong case. He'd see what kind of plea he could get his clients to agree to.

"No deal!" Sergio said positively. "This is far too strong for pleas. We do that when we have doubts. We don't, on this one."

He shrugged, shook hands around and left.

"Well?" Emilio asked, when he was gone. "Is he going to do what you hoped?"

"Iffy, but I think so."

"I'll try to get a quick date for the trial," Sergio suggested. "It probably *could* be today. They aren't very busy. The Thomkins case was the last one that got the higher court's attention, and that one was finished last week. I'll see if we can set Santeriana back another step or two by having a much faster trial than he asked. That was a prod to see if we really thought it was solid. It might help if he doesn't have a lot of time to consider how solid this thing really is. It is, but I'm dying of curiosity about what you have planned."

"Well, so long as everything's presented the way it is on that schedule, it might work. We have the case won, but it could drag with a lot of technicalities Santeriana is known to bring up. I'll just say he thinks he's spotted one hell of a technicality."

Sergio used the phone, then sent Esteban to the courthouse with the outline of the case and the discovery lists. Judge Castile was doing nothing, and called to say they could have the trial as soon as tomorrow at nine thirty, if everyone agreed. He didn't nccd to go through his old court records a fifty first time. Sergio called Santeriana and that was set up. Sergio said his case was so strong that he'd release the prisoners to Santeriana, if he liked. It was on speaker. "So they might try to run and you'd use that to convict them?

"Let them out! They won't get convicted with what you have. They won't be stupid enough to do anything that might make them appear guilty."

Esteban grinned and took the release papers that were already filled out to holding, then brought the two back in. Sergio explained that their lawyer had obtained release in his custody. The trial was tomorrow morning in the courtroom upstairs in the legal building. Their lawyer would be with them. It was trial by a judge, only, their lawyer stating they didn't need the advantage of a jury. They were not to drink any alcoholic beverages, and were to be in their quarters before midnight. No, Goodman would not be allowed to leave the island to sleep in his boat.

They went out as much as congratulating each other. Goodman asked Winston, "Can I pick a lawyer, or can I pick a lawyer?" as they went out. Sergio smirked. Clint giggled.

Tomorrow might be fun!

"Everyone is here present and ready, Your Honor," the bailiff announced, and sat. Judge Castile read over the outline of the case, and said for the police to make a statement, then the defense could make one, if they wished. He grinned at Santeriana and finished, "And I'm most certain Mr. Santeriana will wish to make a long and eloquent statement. Remember that there is no jury to impress here.

"Licenciado?"

The prosecutor stood and asked if Santeriana had read and understood the outline. They would make this as short as they could by stating full understanding of the case. Santeriana said he knew the case very well, indeed. So long as everything listed on discovery was present, they could proceed as stipulated evidence. He went to the evidence table and glanced over it. His eyes paused when he reached one certain item. Clint winked at Sergio.

"We wish to hold this to an informal structure, so will simply let the most qualified among us answer any questions," Lic. Menendez said. "Our case is exactly as was stated. Perhaps we may dispense with direct on much of it?"

"So stated," Santeriana said. "I have one point that makes this a very short proceeding, if I may ask a few questions about one of the items?"

"Proceed. Which item?"

"The supposed murder weapon, a voodoo doll. The theory that it was used to kill anyone is unsupported in court. Voodoo is superstition and the victim must be psychologically weak to mkae it work. Presenting a doll to such as the Partridges and having them die a psychosomatic death is ludicrous. He was a scientist of the first order! My clients have better sense than to do such a thing. They know nothing about any voodoo doll, other than that it was found in their hotel room."

"Mr. Faraday? This was your own personal theory?" Menendez asked.

"Yes. I state unequivocally that anyone who handles that doll is in grave danger of dying."

"How silly!" Santerian said. "How did you bring it here? Mental telepathy?"

"No. It is still in the evidence box, and was never handled by anyone, directly."

"Then I can disprove your ridiculous theory by simply picking it up, myself!" he said and went to the box.

"No! Don't touch it!" Winston yelled. "My god! Larry! He mustn't!"

"No. Don't touch the doll," Goodman said defeatedly. "It will kill you!"

"That is ridiculous! You said you didn't know anything about a voodoo doll!" Santeriana cried, looking at the innocent-seeming doll.

"It's used as a carrier of a fast poison that is absorbed from small needles in the straw," Clint said. "The medical examiner can tell you about it. That it works is demonstrated by the deaths of the Partridges and the reactions of the defendants."

"You actually manipulated me into the position where I would handle the killer doll?" Santeriana asked, shocked.

"No. I manipulated you into saying you would."

"If they hadn't stopped me, I would have. You couldn't stop me."

"Either way, the case is proven. Had they said nothing, you would have handled the doll and died, thereby proving it. If they stopped you, it could only be because handling that doll is fatal, and they knew it. If you died, there would be one less lawyer is all," Doc said.

Santeriana laughed, and said the defense, such as he thought they had, rested.

The judge considered for a moment and said, "In most cases we would have to find which of you committed the act of murder. The reactions of both of you to that piece of evidence makes it painfully clear that you are equally guilty. Your act of murder has taken a good scientific mind and a good woman from us. That is an intolerable act.

"You will both spend a period of fifteen years in the penal institution in Panamá City, after which you will immediately be permanently expelled from this country as undesirables. So stated and recorded. Bailiff, remove the prisoners from this place and transport them to the facility in Panamá City as quickly as is reasonably feasible. Their sentence commences at the moment they are delivered there.

"Next case, if there is one."

There wasn't. He complained that they weren't catching enough of these characters, and their trials weren't taking up enough time to justify his salary – not that he would give up a penny of it. One hour and four minutes must be a record for a double murder trial.

They went back to the station and sat around awhile. Clint went back home and laid around on his deck, went swimming a bit, checked out the computer, and watched a George of the Jungle movie. He thought of how much some of his friends were like the portrayed character. It was exaggerated, and the comedy was added, but the basic character was real to him. He remembered when he looked like that.

Yeah! Like *that* ever happened!

So. Maybe Lily's for a snack, then bum around town awhile, then decide what he would do tonight. He put on fresh shorts and a loose tee shirt and his chankletas, then walked into town. The water taxi was just unloading and Serena, a beautiful girl from Colombia got off. She spotted him and squealed, then ran to hug him and say she was going to spend the night at his place, whether he liked it or not.

He would definitely like it! It was going to be a good night!

C. D. Moulton's works are available on most major outlets as printed or e-books. CD writes the CD Grimes, PI mysteries, the Det. Lt. Nick Storie mysteries, the Clint Faraday mysteries, the Flight of the Maita science fiction series, books on orchid culture and many others of many types. Mystery, adventure, intrigue, science fiction, fantasy, paranormal, mild erotica, and factual.